S0-AHK-466

I Love My Books!

Nathalie Butler

PowerKiDS press.

New York

Published in 2018 by The Rosen Publishing Group, Inc.
29 East 21st Street, New York, NY 10010

Copyright © 2018 by The Rosen Publishing Group, Inc.

All rights reserved. No part of this book may be reproduced in any form without permission in writing from the publisher, except by a reviewer.

First Edition

Book Design: Brian Garvey
Illustrations by Continuum Content Solutions

Cataloging-in-Publication Data
Names: Butler, Nathalie.
Title: I love my books! / Nathalie Butler.
Description: New York : PowerKids Press, 2018. | Series: Learning with stories | Includes index.
Identifiers: ISBN 9781508162452 (pbk.) | ISBN 9781508162476 (library bound) | ISBN 9781508162469 (6 pack) | ISBN 9781508162483 (ebook)
Subjects: LCSH: Books and reading–Juvenile fiction.
Classification: LCC PZ7.I468 2018 | DDC [E]–dc23

CPSIA Compliance Information: Batch #BS17PK: For further information contact Rosen Publishing, New York, New York at 1-800-237-9932

Manufactured in the United States of America

Contents

Are you ready?

It's time to go.

It's time to go to the beach!

Mom is ready.

Grandma
is ready.
I am ready!

Oh no! It's raining!
We can't go!

We can't go to the beach!
What will we do?

Grandma knows what to do.

Mom knows what to do.

I don't know what to do!

Do you?

I want fun!
I want adventure!
I want to go to new places!

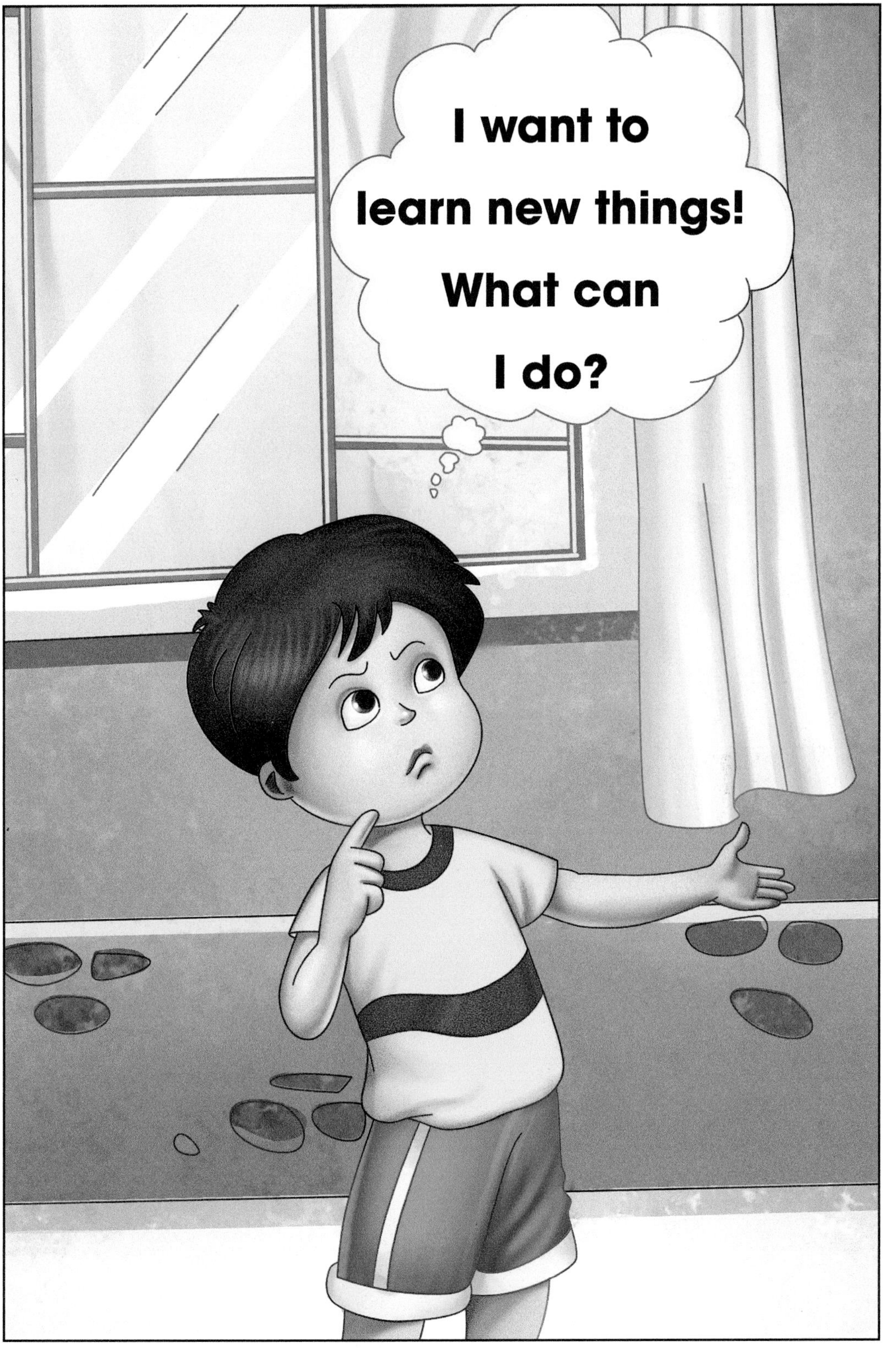
I want to learn new things! What can I do?

Grandma gives me
big books.

Mom gives me small books.

I have so many books!

It's time to read!

I read books to Grandma.

She reads books to me.

We read books about boats.

We read books about butterflies.

We read books about birds, too.

I read books to Mom.

She reads books to me.

We read books about bees.

We read books about bats.

We read books about dinosaur bones, too.

I read books to my dog Bob.

He can't read to me!

Bob likes the book about cats!

Oops! Let go, Bob!

Don't eat the book, Bob!

The rain stopped!

Are you ready?

Are you ready to go to the beach?

It's time to go!

I'm ready!

I'm ready to go to the beach!

The beach is fun. My books are fun, too.

Books at the beach are the best fun!

Words to Know

beach

books

dinosaur

Index